Goldilocks and the Three Bears

Goldilocks and the Three Bears

By

John Batten

Joseph Cundall

Andrew Lang

George Nichol

Robert Southey

Flora Annie Steel

Goldilocks and the Three Bears.

First Printing: 2017.

ISBN: 9781549991042.

Contents

The Eleanor Mure pamphlet

The present day bedtime story of the young girl who disrupts the home life of an anthropomorphic bear family dates in print back to 19th century Great Britain. For a long time Robert Southey's The Story of the Three Bears, first published in 1837, was thought to be the oldest surviving literary version, but then scholars discovered a handwritten copy by a woman named Eleanor Mure dated 1831. In Mure's version an old woman enters the house and tastes the food. A sub-title page of the printed home-made booklet says it's 'The celebrated nursery tale of The Three Bears put into verse and embellished with drawings for a birthday present to Horace Broke' (Mure's nephew). This implies that it was probably based on an earlier oral story. Ms. Mure's version of the fairytale is rather odd. First off, the 'angry old woman' protagonist breaks into the bears' house because they snubbed her during a recent social call. Then in the end when the three 'bachelor' bears catch the old woman, they linger in a long, slow debate over what to do with her. Finally they figure it out:

> On the fire they throw her, but burn her they couldn't;
> In the water they put her, but drown there she wouldn't;
> They seize her before all the wondering people,
> And chuck her aloft on St. Paul's churchyard steeple;
> And if she's still there, when you earnestly look,
> You will see her quite plainly – my dear little Horbook!

*Horbook was the nickname of Eleanor Mure's nephew

The Three Bears by Robert Southey

Although there are references to The Story of the Three Bears in works by Dickens and others that predate its first appearance in print, the fairytale was first recorded in narrative form by British author and poet Robert Southey in 1837.

ONCE upon a time there were three Bears, who lived together in a house of their own in a wood. One of them was a Little, Small, Wee Bear; and one was a Middle-sized Bear, and the other was a Great, Huge Bear. They had each a pot for their porridge, a little pot for the Little, Small, Wee Bear; and a middle-sized pot for the Middle Bear; and a great pot for the Great, Huge Bear. And they had each a chair to sit in: a little chair for the Little, Small, Wee Bear; and a middle-sized chair for the Middle Bear; and a great chair for the Great, Huge Bear. And they had each a bed to sleep in: a little bed for the Little, Small, Wee Bear; and a middle-sized bed for the Middle Bear; and a great bed for the Great, Huge Bear.

One day, after they had made the porridge for their breakfast and poured it into their porridge pots, they walked out into the wood while the porridge was cooling, that they might not burn their mouths by beginning too soon to eat it. And while they were walking a little old woman came to the house. She could not have been a good, honest, old woman; for, first, she looked in at the window, and then she peeped in at the keyhole, and, seeing nobody in the house, she lifted the latch. The door was not fastened, because the bears were good bears, who did nobody any harm, and never suspected that anybody would harm them. So the little old woman opened the door and went in; and well pleased she was when she saw the porridge on the table. If she had been a good little old woman she would have waited till the bears came home, and then, perhaps, they would have asked her to breakfast, for they were good bears; a little rough or so, as the manner of bear's is, but for all that very good-natured and hospitable. But she was an impudent, bad old woman, and set about helping herself.

So first she tasted the porridge of the Great Huge Bear, and that was too hot for her; and she said a bad word about that. And then she tasted the porridge of the Middle Bear, and that was too cold for her; and she said a bad word about that, too. And then she went to the porridge of the Little, Small, Wee Bear, and tasted that, and that was neither too hot nor too cold, but just right; and she liked it so well that she ate it all up; but the naughty old woman said a bad word about the little porridge pot, because it did not hold enough for her.

Then the little old woman sat down in the chair of the Great, Huge Bear, and that was too hard for her. And then she sat down in the chair of the Middle Bear, and that was too soft for her. And then she sat down in the chair of the Little Small, Wee Bear, and that was neither too hard nor too soft, but just right. So she seated herself in it, and there she sat till the bottom of the chair came out, and down came she, plump upon the ground. And the naughty old woman said wicked words about that, too.

Then the little old woman went upstairs into the bedchamber in which the three Bears slept. And first she lay down upon the bed of the Great, Huge Bear, but that was too high at the head for her. And next she lay down upon the bed of the Middle Bear, and that was too high at the foot for her. And then she lay down upon the bed of the Little, Small, Wee Bear, and that was neither too high at the head nor at the foot, but just right. So she covered herself up comfortably, and lay there till she fell asleep. By this time the three Bears thought their porridge would be cool enough, so they came home to breakfast. Now the little old woman had left the spoon of the Great, Huge Bear standing in his porridge.

"SOMEBODY HAS BEEN AT MY PORRIDGE!"

said the Great, Huge Bear, in his great gruff voice. And when the Middle Bear looked at his, he saw that the spoon was standing in it, too. They were wooden spoons; if they had been silver ones the naughty old woman would have put them in her pocket.

"SOMEBODY HAS BEEN AT MY PORRIDGE!" said the middle Bear, in his middle voice.

Then the Little, Small, Wee Bear looked at his, and there was the spoon in the porridge pot, but the porridge was all gone.

"SOMEBODY HAS BEEN AT MY PORRIDGE, AND HAS EATEN IT ALL UP!" said the Little, Small, Wee Bear, in his little, small, wee voice.

Upon this the three Bears, seeing that someone had entered their house and eaten up the Little, Small, Wee Bear's breakfast, began to look about them. Now the little old woman had not put the hard cushion straight when she rose from the chair of the Great, Huge Bear.

"SOMEBODY HAS BEEN SITTING IN MY CHAIR!" said the Great, Huge Bear, in his great, rough, gruff voice.

And the little old woman had squatted down the soft cushion of the Middle Bear.

"SOMEBODY HAS BEEN SITTING IN MY CHAIR!" said the Middle Bear, in his middle voice.

And you know what the little old woman had done to the third chair.

"SOMEBODY HAS BEEN SITTING IN MY CHAIR, AND HAS SAT THE BOTTOM OUT OF IT!"

said the Little, Small, Wee Bear, in his little, small, wee voice.

Then the three bears thought it necessary that they should make further search; so they went upstairs into their bedchamber. Now the little old woman had pulled the pillow of the Great, Huge Bear out of its place.

"SOMEBODY HAS BEEN LYING IN MY BED!" said the Great, Huge Bear, in his great, rough, gruff voice.

And the little old woman had pulled the bolster of the Middle Bear out of its place.

"SOMEBODY HAS BEEN LYING IN MY BED!" said the Middle Bear, in his middle voice.

And when the Little, Small, Wee Bear came to look at his bed, there was the bolster in its place, and upon the pillow was the little old woman's ugly, dirty head-which was not in its place, for she had no business there.

"SOMEBODY HAS BEEN LYING IN MY BED-AND HERE SHE IS!" said the Little, Small, Wee Bear, in his little, small, wee voice.

The little old woman had heard in her sleep the great, rough, gruff voice of the Great, Huge Bear, but she was so fast asleep that it was no more to her than the moaning of wind or the rumbling of thunder. And she had heard the middle voice of the Middle Bear, but it was only as if she had heard someone speaking in a dream. But when she heard the little, small, wee voice of the Little, Small, Wee Bear, it was so sharp and so shrill that it awakened her at once. Up she started, and when she saw the three bears on one side of the bed she tumbled herself out at the other and ran to the window. Now the window was open, because the Bears, like good, tidy bears as they were, always opened their bedchamber window when they got up in the morning. Out the little old woman jumped, and whether she broke her neck in the fall or ran into the wood and was lost there, or found her way out of the wood and was taken up by the constable and sent to the House of Correction for a vagrant as she was, I cannot tell. But the three Bears never saw anything more of her.

The Story of the Three Bears by George Nicol

The same year as Southey's prose form appeared, British writer George Nicol published a version in rhyme based upon Southey's take. Both versions tell of three bears and an old woman who trespasses upon their property. This is the second edition that appeared in 1839.

Three Bears, once on a time did dwell
Snug in a house together,
Which was their own, and suited well
By keeping out the weather.

'Twas seated in a shady wood,
In which they daily walk'd,
And afterwards, as in the mood,
They smok'd and read, or talk'd.

Orie-Ouheni was a great huge bear,
And one of a middle size,
The other a little, small, wee bear,
With small red twinkling eyes.

These Bears, each had a porridge-pot,
From which they used to feed;
The great huge bear's own porridge-pot
Was very large indeed.

A pot of a middle-size, the bear
Of a middle-size had got,
And so the little, small, wee bear,
A little, small, wee pot.

A chair there was for every bear,
When they might choose to sit;
The huge Bear had a great huge chair,
And filled it every bit.

The middle bear a chair had he
Of a middle-size and neat;
The Bear so little, small, and wee
A little, small, wee seat.

They, also, each one had a bed
To sleep upon at night:
The huge bear's was a great, huge bed,
In length, and width and height.

The middle bear laid down his head
On a bed of middle-size;
The wee-bear on a small, wee bed
Did nightly close his eyes.

One morn their porridge being made
And pour'd into each pot,
To taste it they were all afraid
It seem'd so boiling hot.

"A burnt child dreads the fire"... A bear
Doth dread it just as much,
As these Bears proved, in taking care
Their porridge not to touch,

For they most cautious had become
From having once before
Their mouths severely burnt with some,
Which made them dance and roar!

They, therefore, let their breakfast be
Till it should cooler grow-
And meantime for a walk the three
Into the wood did go.

And now a little old woman there
Came, whilst the bears were out;
Through window, keyhole, and everywhere,
She peep'd and peer'd about:

And then she lifted up the latch
And through the door she went.
For hold of all she could to snatch
No doubt was her intent.

The Bears had left the door undone
While strolling in the wood,
For they suspected harm from none
They were, themselves, so good.

The little old Dame had entered in,
And was well pleased to find
The porridge-pots, and that within
They held food of small kind.

Now had she waited till home came
The, Bears, most likely, they
To breakfast might have asked the Dame,
And begg'd of her to stay.

But she was impudent and bold,
And cared for none a pin;
So quickly of a spoon laid hold
The porridge to dip in.

And first out of the great Bear's pot
The porridge she did taste,
Which proving to be very hot
She spat it out in haste.

She burn'd her mouth, at which half mad
She said a naughty word;
A naughty word it was and bad,
As ever could be heard.
The middle bear's she tasted next,
Which being rather cold,
She disappointed was, and vext,
And with bad words did scold.

But now to where the small, wee bear
Had left his small, wee cup

She came, and soon the porridge there
By her was eaten up.

A wicked word she spoke again
As wicked as before,
Because this pot did not contain
Many a spoonful more.

Then down the little old woman sat
Within the huge Bear's chair,
But much too hard for her was that,
And so she staid not there.

Next she tried the middle-sized one
And that too soft she found
Then sat the small, wee chair upon,
Which fitted her all round.

Now here for sometime sat the Dame
Till half inclined to snore,
When out this wee chair's bottom came
And her's came on the floor

A wicked word about this too
She spoke-then went up-stairs,
And poked her ugly head into
The bed-room of the Bears.

And down upon the huge Bear's bed
She lay, which was too high
To suit her little ugly bead,
Which easy could not lie.

Then to the middle Bear's she goes
And quick upon it got,
But at the foot too high it rose,
And so she liked it not.

Now down upon the small wee bed
She lay, and it was quite
The thing, both at the foot and head,

And fitted her just right.

Thus finding that it suited well
Within the clothes she crept;
Then soon into a slumber fell
And snug and soundly slept.

Although the morning sun shone bright
And birds did sweetly sing,
She' slept, as if it had been night,
This sad, old, lazy thing.

The three Bears in their jackets rough
Now came in from the wood,
Thinking their porridge long enough
To cool itself had stood.

"Somebody has at my porridge been!"
The huge Bear's gruff voice cried;
For there the spoon was sticking in,
Which he left at the side.

"Somebody has at my porridge been!"
Then said the middle Bear,
For also in his pot was seen
The spoon, which made him stare.

These spoons were wooden spoons, not made
Of silver, else full soon
This wicked Dame would, I'm afraid,
Have pocketed each spoon.

The small bear's small voice said, as in
He peer'd to his wee cup,
"Somebody has at my porridge been,
And eaten it all up!"

On this the three Bears finding that
The while they had been out,
Someone the door had entered at,
Began to look about.

"Somebody in my chair has sat!"
With voice so gruff and great
The huge bear said, when he saw that
His cushion was not straight.

"Somebody in my chair has been!"
The middle Bear exclaim'd;
Seeing the cushion dinted in
By what may not be named.

Then said the little-small wee bear,
"Someone's been sitting in my chair!"

Now having search'd the house below
Most prudently these bears,
Thought it just as well to go
And do the same up-stairs.
"Some one's been lying in my bed!"
Cried out the great huge Bear,
Who left his pillow at the head
And now it was not there.

"Some one's been lying in my bed!"
The middle Bear then cried,
For it was tumbled at the head
And at the foot and side.

And now the little wee bear said
With voice both small and shrill,
"Some one's been lying in my bed,
And here she's lying still."

The other bears look'd at the bed,
And on the pillow-case
They saw her li dirty head
And little ugly face.

The little old woman had the deep
Voice of the huge Bear heard,
But she was in so sound a sleep

She neither woke nor stirr'd:

For it appear'd to her no more
Than thunder rumbling by,
Or than the angry winds, which roar,
And sweep along the sky.

And she had heard the middle Bear,
Whose middle voice did seem
To her asleep, as though it were
The voice but of a dream.

But when the small, wee Bear did speak,
She started up in bed,
His voice it was so shrill, the squealer
Shot through her ugly head.

She rubb'd her eyes, and when she saw
The three Bears at her side,
She sprang full quick upon the floor-
And then with hop and stride

She to the open window flew,
Which these good tidy bears
Wide open every morning threw,
When shaved they went down stairs.

She leapt out with a sudden bound,
And whether in her fall
She broke her neck upon the ground,
Or was not hurt at all,
Or whether to the wood she tied
And amongst trees was lost,
Or found a path which straightway led
To where the highways cross'd,
And there was by the Beadle caught
And taken into jail
This sad old woman good naught!
Remains an untold tale.

Scrapefoot (An English Tale) by John Batten

John Batten, a prolific illustrator of folktale and fairytale collections, contributed a story to Joseph Jacobs' More English Fairy Tales of 1894 (Jacobs had included Southey's story of the Three Bears in a previous volume of English Fairy Tales). Batten's story, Scrapefoot, is recognizable as a version of the story of the Three Bears in which the protagonist is neither a little girl nor an old lady but a fox. It's possible that this story predates Southey's version in the oral tradition. Southey may have heard "Scrapefoot", and confused its 'vixen' with a synonym for an unpleasant, malicious old woman. Some maintain however that the story as well as the old woman originated with Southey.

ONCE upon a time, there were three Bears who lived in a castle in a great wood. One of them was a great big Bear, and one was a middling Bear, and one was a little Bear. And in the same wood there was a Fox who lived all alone, his name was Scrapefoot. Scrapefoot was very much afraid of the Bears, but for all that he wanted very much to know all about them.

And one day as he went through the wood he found himself near the Bears' castle, and he wondered whether he could get into the castle. He looked all about him everywhere, and he could not see anyone. So he came up very quietly, till at last he came up to the door of the castle, and he tried whether he could open it.

Yes! the door was not locked, and he opened it just a little way, and put his nose in and looked, and he could not see anyone. So then he opened it a little way farther, and put one paw in, and then another paw, and another and another, and then he was all in the Bears' castle. He found he was in a great hail with three chairs in it — one big, one middling, and one little chair; and he thought he would like to sit down and rest and look about him; so he sat down on the big chair.

But he found it so hard and uncomfortable that it made his bones ache, and he jumped down at once and got into the middling chair, and he turned round and round in it, but he couldn't make himself comfortable. So then he went to the little chair and sat down in it, and it was so soft and warm and comfortable that Scrapefoot was quite happy; but all at once it broke to pieces under him and he couldn't put it together again! So he got up and began to look about him again, and on one table he saw three saucers, of which one was very big, one was middling, one was quite a little saucer. Scrapefoot was very thirsty, and he began to drink out of the big saucer. But he only just tasted the milk in the big saucer, which was so sour and so nasty that he would not taste another drop of it. Then he tried the middling saucer, and he drank a little of that. He tried two or three mouthfuls, but it was not nice, and then he left it and went to the little saucer, and the milk in the little saucer was so sweet and so nice that he went on drinking it till it was all gone.

Then Scrapefoot thought he would like to go upstairs; and he listened and he could not hear anyone. So upstairs he went, and he found a great room with three beds in it; one was a big bed, and one was a middling bed, and one was a little white bed; and he climbed up into the big bed, but it was so hard and lumpy and uncomfortable that he jumped down again at once, and tried the middling bed. That was rather better, but he could not get comfortable in it, so after turning about a little while he got up and went to the little bed; and that was so soft and so warm and so nice that he fell fast asleep at once.

And after a time the Bears came home, and when they got into the hail the big Bear went to his chair and said,

'WHO'S BEEN SITTING IN MY CHAIR?'

and the middling Bear said,

'WHO'S BEEN SITTING IN MY CHAIR?'

and the little Bear said,
'Who's been sitting in my chair and has broken it all to pieces?'
And then they went to have their milk, and the big Bear said,
'WHO'S BEEN DRINKING MY MILK?'
and the middling Bear said,
'WHO'S BEEN DRINKING MY MILK?'
and the little Bear said,
'Who's been drinking my milk and has drunk it all up?'
Then they went upstairs and into the bedroom, and the big Bear said,
'WHO'S BEEN SLEEPING IN MY BED?'
and the middling Bear said,
'WHO'S BEEN SLEEPING IN MY BED?'
and the little Bear said,
'Who's been sleeping in my bed? — and see here he is!'
So then the Bears came and wondered what they should do with him; and the big Bear said, 'Let's hang him!' and then the middling Bear said, 'Let's drown him!' and then the little Bear said, 'Let's throw him out of the window.' And then the Bears took him to the window, and the big Bear took two legs on one side and the middling Bear took two legs on the other side, and they swung him backwards and forwards, backwards and forwards, and out of the window. Poor Scrapefoot was so frightened, and he thought every bone in his body must be broken. But he got up and first shook one leg — no, that was not broken; and then another, and that was not broken; and another and another, and then he wagged his tail and found there were no bones broken. So then he galloped off home as fast as he could go, and never went near the Bears' castle again.

Silver-hair and the Three Bears by Joseph Cundall

Southey's tale was immediately seized on for adaptation by other authors. In the years which followed, it was rewritten repeatedly for eager audiences, becoming the tale we recognize today. The first author to make the protagonist a young girl was apparently Joseph Cundall, a pioneer publisher of children's books and also notable as a pioneer photographer; he did it for his 1849 Treasury of Pleasure Books for Young Children. Cundall gave the little girl silver hair and a name to match – fashionable choices for Victorian heroines – and this set the trend for half a century or so; he also seems to have been the one who turned the middle bear female.

In a far-off country there was once a little girl who was called Silver-hair, because her curly hair shone brightly. She was a sad romp, and so restless that she could not be kept quiet at home, but must needs run out and away, without leave.

One day she started off into a wood to gather wild flowers, and into the fields to chase butterflies. She ran here and she ran there, and went so far, at last, that she found herself in a lonely place, where she saw a snug little house, in which three bears lived; but they were not then at home.

The door was ajar, and Silver-hair pushed it open and found the place to be quite empty, so she made up her mind to go in boldly, and look all about the place, little thinking what sort of people lived there.

Now the three bears had gone out to walk a little before this. They were the Big Bear, and the Middle-sized Bear, and the Little Bear; but they had left their porridge on the table to cool. So when Silver-hair came into the kitchen, she saw the three bowls of porridge. She tasted the largest bowl, which belonged to the Big Bear, and found it too cold; then she tasted the middle-sized bowl, which belonged to the Middle-sized Bear, and found it too hot; then she tasted the smallest bowl, which belonged to the Little Bear, and it was just right, and she ate it all.

She went into the parlour, and there were three chairs. She tried the biggest chair, which belonged to the Big Bear, and found it too high; then she tried the middle-sized chair, which belonged to the Middle-sized Bear, and she found it too broad; then she tried the little chair, which belonged to the Little Bear, and found it just right, but she sat in it so hard that she broke it.

Now Silver-hair was by this time very tired, and she went upstairs to the chamber, and there she found three beds. She tried the largest bed, which belonged to the Big Bear, and found it too soft; then she tried the middle-sized bed, which belonged to the Middle-sized Bear, and she found it too hard; then she tried the smallest bed, which belonged to the Little Bear, and found it just right, so she lay down upon it, and fell fast asleep.

While Silver-hair was lying fast asleep, the three bears came home from their walk. They came into the kitchen, to get their porridge, but when the Big Bear went to his, he growled out:

"SOMEBODY HAS BEEN TASTING MY PORRIDGE!"

and the Middle-sized Bear looked into his bowl, and said:

"Somebody Has Been Tasting My Porridge!"

and the Little Bear piped:

"Somebody has tasted my porridge and eaten it all up!"

Then they went into the parlour, and the Big Bear growled:

"SOMEBODY HAS BEEN SITTING IN MY CHAIR!"

and the Middle-sized Bear said:

"Somebody Has Been Sitting In My Chair!"

and the Little Bear piped:

"Somebody has been sitting in my chair, and has broken it all to pieces!"

So they went upstairs into the chamber, and the Big Bear growled:

"SOMEBODY HAS BEEN TUMBLING MY BED!"

and the Middle-sized Bear said:

"Somebody Has Been Tumbling My Bed!"

and the little Bear piped:

"Somebody has been tumbling my bed, and here she is!"

At that, Silver-hair woke in a fright, and jumped out of the window and ran away as fast as her legs could carry her, and never went near the Three Bears' snug little house again.

The Three Bears by Andrew Lang

Folklorist Andrew Lang based his 1892 version of the tale on Robert Southey's version from 1837.

ONCE upon a time there were Three Bears, who lived together in a house of their own in a wood. One of them was a Little, Small, Wee Bear; and one was a Middle-sized Bear, and the other was a Great, Huge Bear. They had each a pot for their porridge, a little pot for the Little, Small, Wee Bear; and a middle-sized pot for the Middle Bear; and a great pot for the Great, Huge Bear. And they had each a chair to sit in; a little chair for the Little, Small, Wee Bear; and a middle-sized chair for the Middle Bear; and a great chair for the Great, Huge Bear. And they had each a bed to sleep in; a little bed for the Little, Small, Wee Bear; and a middle- sized bed for the Middle Bear; and a great bed for the Great, Huge Bear.

One day, after they had made the porridge for their breakfast, and poured it into their porridge-pots, they walked out into the wood while the porridge was cooling, that they might not burn their mouths by beginning too soon to eat it. And while they were walking, a little old woman came to the house. She could not have been a good, honest old woman; for, first, she looked in at the window, and then she peeped in at the keyhole; and, seeing nobody in the house, she lifted the latch. The door was not fastened, because the bears were good bears, who did nobody any harm, and never suspected that anybody would harm them. So the little old woman opened the door and went in; and well pleased she was when she saw the porridge on the table. If she had been a good little old woman she would have waited till the bears came home, and then, perhaps, they would have asked her to breakfast; for they were good bears-a little rough or so, as the manner of bears is, but for all that very good-natured and hospitable. But she was an impudent, bad old woman, and set about helping herself.

So first she tasted the porridge of the Great, Huge Bear, and that was too hot for her; and she said a bad word about that. And then he tasted the porridge of the Middle Bear; and that was too cold for her; and she said a bad word about that too. And then she went to the porridge of the Little, Small, Wee Bear, and tasted that; and that was neither too hot nor too cold, but just right; and she liked it so well, that she ate it all up: but the naughty old woman said bad word about the little porridge-pot, because it did not hold enough for her.

Then the little old woman sate down in the chair of the Great, Huge Bear, and that was too hard for her. And then she sat down in the chair of the Middle Bear, and that was too soft for her. And then she sat down in the chair of the Little, Small, Wee Bear, and that was neither too hard nor too soft, but just right. So she seated herself in it, and there she sate till the bottom of the chair came out, and down came she, plump upon the ground. And the naughty old woman said a wicked word about that too.

Then the little old woman went upstairs into the bed-chamber in which the three bears slept. And first she lay down upon the bed of the Great, Huge Bear; but that was too high at the head for her. And next she lay down upon the bed of the Middle Bear; and that was too high at the foot for her. And then she lay down upon the bed of the Little, Small, Wee Bear; and that was neither too high at the head, nor at the foot, but just right. So she covered herself up comfortably, and lay there till she fell fast asleep.

By this time the three bears thought their porridge would be cool enough; so they came home to breakfast. Now the little old woman had left the spoon of the Great, Huge Bear, standing in his porridge.

'SOMEBODY HAS BEEN AT MY PORRIDGE!'

said the Great, Huge Bear, in his great gruff voice. And when the Middle Bear looked at his, he saw that the spoon was standing in it too. They were wooden spoons; if they had been silver ones, the naughty old woman would have put them in her pocket.

'SOMEBODY HAS BEEN AT MY PORRIDGE!'

said the Middle Bear, in his middle voice.

Then the Little, Small, Wee Bear looked at his, and there was the spoon in the porridge-pot, but the porridge was all gone.

'Somebody has been at my porridge, and has eaten it all up!'

said the Little, Small Wee Bear, in his little, small wee voice,

Upon this the three bears, seeing that someone had entered their house, and eaten up the Little, Small Wee Bear's breakfast began to look about them. Now the little old woman had not put the hard cushion straight when she rose from the chair of the Great, Huge Bear.

'SOMEBODY HAS BEEN SITTING IN MY CHAIR!

said the Great, Huge Bear, in his great, rough, gruff voice. And the little old woman had squatted down the soft cushion of the Middle Bear.

'SOMEBODY HAS BEEN SITTING IN MY CHAIR!'

said the Middle Bear, in his middle voice.

And you know what the little old woman had done to the third chair.

'Somebody has been sitting in my chair, and has sate the bottom of it out!'

said the Little. Small, Wee Bear, in his little, small, wee voice.

Then the three bears thought it necessary that they should make farther search; so they went upstairs into their bed-chamber. Now the little old woman had pulled the pillow of the Great, Huge Bear out of its place.

'SOMEBODY HAS BEEN LYING IN MY BED!'

said the Great, Huge Bear, in his great, rough, gruff voice. And the little old woman had pulled the bolster of the Middle Bear out of its place.

'SOMEBODY HAS BEEN LYING IN MY BED!'

said the Middle Bear in his middle voice.

And when the Little, Small, Wee Bear came to look at his bed, there was the bolster in its place, and the pillow in its place upon the bolster, and upon the pillow was the little old woman's ugly, dirty head,--which was not in its place, for she had no business there.

'Somebody has been lying in my bed, and here she is!'

said the Little, Small, Wee Bear, in his little, small, wee voice.

The little old woman had heard in her sleep the great, rough, gruff voice of the Great, Huge Bear; but she was so fast asleep that it was no more to her than the roaring of wind or the rumbling of thunder. And she had heard the middle voice of the Middle Bear, but it was only as if she had heard someone speaking in a dream. But when she heard the little, small, wee voice of the Little, Small, Wee bear, it was so sharp, and so shrill, that it awakened her at once. Up she started; and when she saw the Three Bears on one side of the bed, she tumbled herself out at the other, and ran to the window. Now the window was open, because the bears, like good, tidy bears as they were, always opened their bedchamber window when they got up in the morning. Out the little old woman jumped; and whether she broke her neck in the fall, or ran into the wood and was lost there, or found her way out of the wood and was taken up by the constable and sent to the House of Correction for a vagrant as she was, I cannot tell. But the Three Bears never saw anything more of her.

The Story of the Three Bears by Flora Annie Steel

In 1858, Aunt Mavor's Nursery Tales for Good Little People altered the name of the girl protagonist from Silver-hair to Silverlocks. In 1868, in Aunt Friendly's Nursery Book, the name changed again, this time to Golden Hair. In 1889 she became Little Golden-Hair. Finally, over 50 years after the little girl is introduced, in 1904 we get... GOLDILOCKS in Old Nursery Stories and Rhymes with credit to Flora Annie Steel.

Once upon a time there were three Bears, who lived together in a house of their own, in a wood. One of them was a Little Wee Bear, and one was a Middle-sized Bear, and the other was a Great Big Bear. They had each a bowl for their porridge; a little bowl for the Little Wee Bear; and a middle-sized bowl for the Middle-sized Bear; and a great bowl for the Great Big Bear. And they had each a chair to sit in; a little chair for the Little Wee Bear; and a middle-sized chair for the Middle-sized Bear; and a great chair for the Great Big Bear. And they had each a bed to sleep in; a little bed for the Little Wee Bear; and a middle-sized bed for the Middle-sized Bear; and a great bed for the Great Big Bear.

One day, after they had made the porridge for their breakfast, and poured it into their porridge-bowls, they walked out into the wood while the porridge was cooling, that they might not burn their mouths by beginning too soon, for they were polite, well-brought-up Bears. And while they were away a little girl called Goldilocks, who lived at the other side of the wood and had been sent on an errand by her mother, passed by the house, and looked in at the window. And then she peeped in at the keyhole, for she was not at all a well-brought-up little girl. Then seeing nobody in the house she lifted the latch. The door was not fastened, because the Bears were good Bears, who did nobody any harm, and never suspected that anybody would harm them. So Goldilocks opened the door and went in; and well pleased was she when she saw the porridge on the table. If she had been a well-brought-up little girl she would have waited till the Bears came home, and then, perhaps, they would have asked her to breakfast; for they were good Bears – a little rough or so, as the manner of Bears is, but for all that very good-natured and hospitable. But she was an impudent, rude little girl, and so she set about helping herself.

First she tasted the porridge of the Great Big Bear, and that was too hot for her. Next she tasted the porridge of the Middle-sized Bear, but that was too cold for her. And then she went to the porridge of the Little Wee Bear, and tasted it, and that was neither too hot nor too cold, but just right, and she liked it so well that she ate it all up, every bit!

Then Goldilocks, who was tired, for she had been catching butterflies instead of running on her errand, sat down in the chair of the Great Big Bear, but that was too hard for her. And then she sat down in the chair of the Middle-sized Bear, and that was too soft for her. But when she sat down in the chair of the Little Wee Bear, that was neither too hard nor too soft, but just right. So she seated herself in it, and there she sate till the bottom of the chair came out, and down she came, plump upon the ground; and that made her very cross, for she was a bad-tempered little girl.

Now, being determined to rest, Goldilocks went upstairs into the bed-chamber in which the Three Bears slept. And first she lay down upon the bed of the Great Big Bear, but that was too high at the head for her. And next she lay down upon the bed of the Middle-sized Bear, and that was too high at the foot for her. And then she lay down upon the bed of the Little Wee Bear, and that was neither too high at the head nor at the foot, but just right. So she covered herself up comfortably, and lay there till she fell fast asleep.

By this time the Three Bears thought their porridge would be cool enough for them to eat it properly; so they came home to breakfast. Now careless Goldilocks had left the spoon of the Great Big Bear standing in his porridge.

"SOMEBODY HAS BEEN AT MY PORRIDGE!" said the Great Big Bear in his great, rough, gruff voice.

Then the Middle-sized Bear looked at his porridge and saw the spoon was standing in it too.

"SOMEBODY HAS BEEN AT MY PORRIDGE!" said the Middle-sized Bear in his middle-sized voice.

Then the Little Wee Bear looked at his, and there was the spoon in the porridge-bowl, but the porridge was all gone!

"SOMEBODY HAS BEEN AT MY PORRIDGE, AND HAS EATEN IT ALL UP!" said the Little Wee Bear in his little wee voice.

Upon this the Three Bears, seeing that someone had entered their house, and eaten up the Little Wee Bear's breakfast, began to look about them. Now the careless Goldilocks had not put the hard cushion straight when she rose from the chair of the Great Big Bear.

"SOMEBODY HAS BEEN SITTING IN MY CHAIR!" said the Great Big Bear in his great, rough, gruff voice.

And the careless Goldilocks had squatted down the soft cushion of the Middle-sized Bear.

"SOMEBODY HAS BEEN SITTING IN MY CHAIR!" said the Middle-sized Bear in his middle-sized voice.

"SOMEBODY HAS BEEN SITTING IN MY CHAIR, AND HAS SATE THE BOTTOM THROUGH!" said the Little Wee Bear in his little wee voice.

Then the Three Bears thought they had better make further search in case it was a burglar, so they went upstairs into their bedchamber. Now Goldilocks had pulled the pillow of the Great Big Bear out of its place.

"SOMEBODY HAS BEEN LYING IN MY BED!" said the Great Big Bear in his great, rough, gruff voice.

And Goldilocks had pulled the bolster of the Middle-sized Bear out of its place.

"SOMEBODY HAS BEEN LYING IN MY BED!" said the Middle-sized Bear in his middle-sized voice.

But when the Little Wee Bear came to look at his bed, there was the bolster in its place!

And the pillow was in its place upon the bolster!

And upon the pillow − − ?

There was Goldilocks's yellow head − which was not in its place, for she had no business there.

"SOMEBODY HAS BEEN LYING IN MY BED, − AND HERE SHE IS STILL!" said the Little Wee Bear in his little wee voice.

Now Goldilocks had heard in her sleep the great, rough, gruff voice of the Great Big Bear; but she was so fast asleep that it was no more to her than the roaring of wind, or the rumbling of thunder. And she had heard the middle-sized voice of the Middle-sized Bear, but it was only as if she had heard someone speaking in a dream. But when she heard the little wee voice of the Little Wee Bear, it was so sharp, and so shrill, that it awakened her at once. Up she started, and when she saw the Three Bears on one side of the bed, she tumbled herself out at the other, and ran to the window. Now the window was open, because the Bears, like good, tidy Bears, as they were, always opened their bedchamber window when they got up in the morning. So naughty, frightened little Goldilocks jumped; and whether she broke her neck in the fall, or ran into the wood and was lost there, or found her way out of the wood and got whipped for being a bad girl and playing truant, no one can say. But the Three Bears never saw anything more of her.

Made in the USA
Las Vegas, NV
08 May 2022

48595685R00021